GOOD KNIGHT

Linda R. Rymill

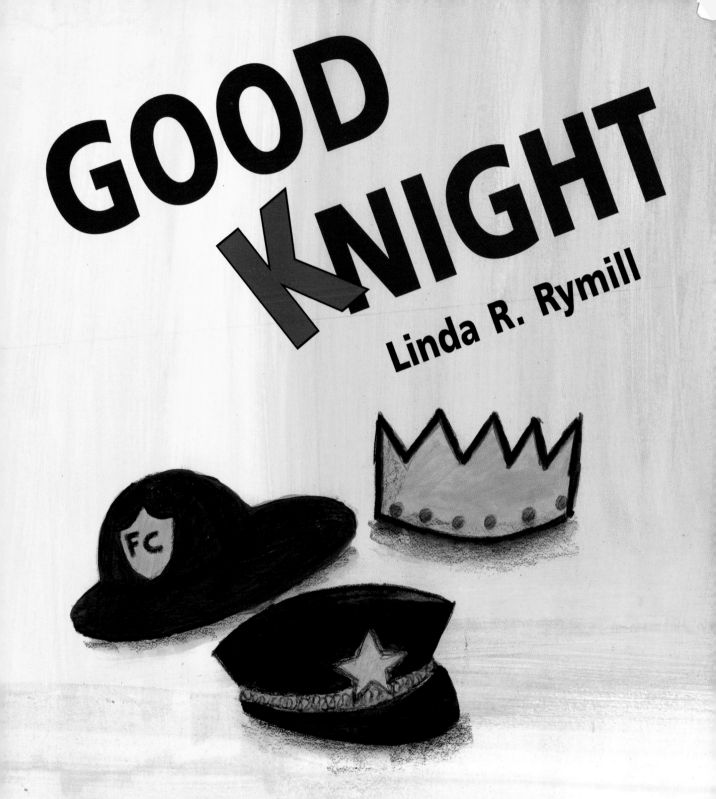

illustrated by G. Brian Karas

Henry Holt and Company • New York

For Kyle, my inspiration, and Jessi,
my "Good Knight" — L.R.

For Bennett, our bedtime battler —B.K.

"No. You can't make me.

I don't want a bath I say.
I'm busy putting flames out.

I'm **Fire Chief** today.

Besides, I have to save the cat;
she's stuck up in this tree.

And I can almost reach her.

Hey,
let go
of
me!

Don't take my boots. That's my hose.

I can't be Chief
without my clothes.

I **won't** feel better 'afterward,'
no matter what you say.

I don't want to play tomorrow,

I want to play today.

I can't sail
my boats in bubbles.

You're getting the shampoo?

Target sighted—and in range.
Missile launch: On two.
Admiral to Navy: Calling in all troops.
Battle stations, ready?

CHUUUUU!

Oops.
No.
You can't make me.

I'm not through yet I say.
I hardly even started.

Please? I want to stay.

No. Don't get the pink towel.
Admirals don't **use** pink.

You're rubbing off my
stripes and **stars**

and **even skin,** I think.

Pajamas? But it's not that time!

I'll wear this robe instead.

And I will rule my kingdom
with a **crown** upon my head.

you'll fall into my moat.

It's filled with **hungry creatures** and you don't have a boat.

I won't and **you can't make me.**

Give me back my crown!
You can't invade my castle.
The drawbridge **isn't down.**

Oh ple-ease no. Don't kiss me.

I'm covering my head.

Don't say good night.

I won't 'sleep tight.'

It isn't time for bed!

You forgot to fluff my pillow!
You forgot my night-light, too.

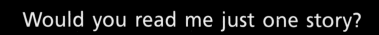

Would you read me just one story?

Momma,

I love you."

Henry Holt and Company, Inc., *Publishers since 1866*
115 West 18th Street New York, New York 10011

Henry Holt is a registered trademark of Henry Holt and Company, Inc.

Published in Canada by Fitzhenry & Whiteside Ltd.,
195 Allstate Parkway, Markham, Ontario L3R 4T8.

Library of Congress Cataloging-in-Publication Data
Rymill, Linda.
Good knight / Linda Rymill; illustrated by Brian Karas.
Summary: A child insists that he is a fire chief, an admiral,
and a king in order to delay going to bed.
[1. Beditme—Fiction. 2. Mother and child—Fiction.]
I. Karas, Brian, ill. II. Title. PZ7.R984Go 1997 [E]—dc21 97-18665

ISBN 0-8050-4129-X First Edition—1998
Designed by Meredith Baldwin
The artist used gouache, acrylic, and pencil on paper to create the illustrations for this book.

Printed in the United States of America on acid-free paper. ∞
1 3 5 7 9 10 8 6 4 2